First Lady

The Truth Shall Set You Free

First Lady

The Truth Shall Set You Free

Rochelle Pearson

Copyright

Printed in the United States of America
First Printing, 2018

ISBN 978-1-947656-59-8
ISBN10: 1947656597

Butterfly Typeface Publishing
PO Box 56193
Little Rock, AR 72215

www.butterflytypeface.com

Dedication

*For my grandmother
who encouraged me to be a First Lady,
not to a Pastor,
but to my Heavenly Father.*

"I guess it's true what they say;

the truth shall set you free."

Table of Contents

Foreword

I believe I was 'destined' to publish this book.

Long before I knew of Rochelle Pearson, I was introduced to a First Lady. We became great friends and she trusted me with information and feelings that she hadn't previously shared. Later she and I took a journey together where I found myself in the midst of a "First Lady" convention. As I sat there thinking, "I don't belong here. I'm not a First Lady," I got this overwhelming sense of a belonging. I realized I did belong and I was indeed a First Lady even though I wasn't married to a pastor.

What I've learned is that being a First Lady is a calling, a mindset, an obligation; not to the pastor or even to the congregation, but to God. A First Lady must be a servant to God, to her husband (if she's married), and not the least of which, to the people she has been called to inspire, encourage, and feed spiritually.

So you see, by the time I met Rochelle Pearson, I was prepared to publish this book.

This book is entertaining. It is shocking. But more than that, it will leave you with a sense of knowing and understanding. When you walk away from this book (and into the journal), I hope that you will have found what I found – a sense of purpose.

I believe it is the job of each of us to put away the stones we would throw and instead throw an empathetic arm around our sister when she is hurting and in need of an Earthly Angel.

Behind every big hat, flashy smile and gloved hand beats the heart of a woman just like you and me. This woman, though called to lead, serve and shepherd, sometimes needs to be able to be vulnerable. She needs a soft place to land. She needs to be heard and sometimes she may even need to cry.

If that woman is you, allow yourself to be loved. If that woman is someone you know – love her unconditionally.

Thank you, Rochelle Pearson, for allowing me to assist with your work and for shedding light in a place where darkness threatens to abide.

Oris M. Williams

Author/Publisher

Acknowledgments

To the First Lady,

Rest your hat and gloves; make yourself
at home ...

R. Pearson

Prelude

This is the story of three women whose desire to be First Lady proved that all that glittered was not gold as once told.

Realization from the attention, the glamour, and the fame that accompanies being a First Lady came to a head. Each woman soon realized that being a First Lady was not all it was cracked up to be. The lies, deceit, the hurt, and the pain that come with being a First Lady forced them to face reality.

The defeats and triumphs of their story will highlight things in your life and help you to see your true self.

At the end of the day, one has to be true to self. Be you, live you, and do you in the truth and the spirit of life.

Pastor David
&
First Lady Monica Moore

First Lady Monica
Acting in Church

I think I was about nine-years-old when I was first exposed to some 'truth.' Penny and I were playing in church, and Big Mama came over to chastise us.

"Stop talking and close your legs," she said firmly. "This is NOT how young ladies ought to act in church!"

Neither of us bothered to respond.

"How in the world you both are going to be First Ladies one day?" Then, she held out her hand, and we knew we'd been caught.

We both spat out our bubblegum that we'd been chewing and placed it in Big Mama's hand. She pulled a tissue out of her pocketbook and wrapped the chewed gum in it.

Penny and I stopped talking, sat up straight, and began to listen to what Pastor was saying.

I didn't know it then, but I was being groomed to become a First Lady. I didn't want that.

From what I could see, the First Lady just sat up front with her fancy dresses, big hats, gloves, and shoes to match. Don't talk about her pocketbook; it always matched her shoes and the color of whatever she wore. It seemed like when The Spirit was in the church, she didn't even feel it. I guess it was all the fanciness she had on that made The Holy Spirit unable to get to her. She didn't even clap her hands!

I loved church growing up, especially the singing! Boy when there was a good song sung, I got happy and wasn't afraid of who saw me. Me being First Lady, no way!

Twenty years have passed since that day of revelation.

I went away to college, received a Master's in Education, and never stopped going to church while I was in college. I was in the big city of New York, and it seemed like there was a church on every corner, not to mention a liquor store was on every corner as well. I never became a member of any church while I was there. I just hopped from church to church. I would get up on Sunday mornings and just take a train ride. I would randomly get off the train, walk out of the subway, and whatever church I came to first was the one I'd attend.

I would sit in the back and just observe the way the people would worship. Some churches were very strange to me, and I wouldn't stay long. I would leave quietly and end up in Prospect Park for the rest of the day, especially if it was a nice day outside.

There was one church I did like attending. It was a big church in Harlem. The original art work and stained-glass windows were amazing to me. They even had a black Jesus painting hanging in the vestibule. I had never seen anything like it. At my church down home, we had always had a white Jesus hanging on the wall alongside Dr. Martin Luther King Jr. and President

John F. Kennedy. When I was younger, I thought they were the Father, Son and Holy Spirit. At the time, I never quite figured out which one was which.

It was different for me to have attended such a large church in a big city. The styles of dress were even different, very high end and fancy clothing both for the men and women.

After a while, I just fell into the flow.

Even the preaching was different, something like high tech, mega still preaching which meant no "huh," after every word. Most of all they did not sing any foot stomping, hand clapping hymns. They did not sing the kind of songs without music. These kinds of songs made a person feel as if he or she was moaning and back on the plantation.

People came and went without speaking, and it was clear that no one knew each other. I was not used to that. In my home church, down in the small town of Timmonsville, SC, *everyone* knew each other.

I liked this new way of worshipping because I knew nobody would be in my business. Big city living was going to be my thing.

I learned so much in the city.

The culture that Harlem had to offer was breathtaking. I was never much of a night life person, but the city begged to be explored. The food, the people, and the New York attitude were in a culture all by themselves.

There where African people actually living in New York. Africans who *actually* came from Africa *recently*. They owned businesses but could hardly speak English. Nevertheless, we understood each other enough.

I loved the arts. There were plays that portrayed blacks in leading roles.

The dance theater of Harlem showcased some powerful dancers. The Schomburg Center, where a lot of black history is found, is where I learned a lot about our black history along with our rich heritage. I learned about our Native American and Spanish brothers and sisters as well.

I lived in a brownstone building in Brooklyn. Brooklyn had a culture of its own. There were so many black people who were from so many different places that I had never heard of: the Caribbean, South America, and Central America.

Whatever country you named, Brooklyn had them living there. To me, Brooklyn was a country in and of itself.

My apartment was on the 1st floor in the back of the building. There was not much to the area behind my apartment, but we called it the backyard. It was actually a concrete slab about 10 by 12 in diameter. The building was three stories, and the other tenants and I sure made use of the backyard. If space ran out in the back, we just took whatever event we were having to the front yard which was the sidewalk.

Boy, when we had a party, we never ran out of food, but if we did, the corner store was right on the corner and stayed open all night. We could buy whatever we needed. You could even buy beer on a Sunday. Oh my! I know some of my kinfolk would have loved that.

I dated off and on while I was in New York. It was nothing serious, although I had opportunities to get married, but my heart was never in it.

Big Mama died, and I found myself thinking about down home more. I loved the city life, and I was determined to make it work. Whenever I thought about going home, my next thought would be, "What could I possibly do if I did go back down home?" I just knew that New York was going to be my home, but God had another plan for me.

My college years and living in New York were now just fond memories.

These days, I can be found on Sunday mornings, sitting up front at church, wearing fancy dresses, big hats with the gloves, and shoes to match. Yes, I had the pocket book to match too!

My husband, David Moore, is a Pastor. Yes, that makes me *Mrs. Moore*, First *Lady Moore*. I guess Big Mama knew more than I thought she did. She didn't live to see me get married. She had died while I was still in New York.

I knew David growing up. His father was a Pastor at another church that our church fellowshipped with from time to time. David played the piano for his church, and I sung in the choir at my church. When we were younger, he used to tell me that we were going to get married. Who me? I didn't want to marry a preacher's kid. You know what they say about PK's.

David went to college and got his PhD in Theology. I guess he really knows The

Bible now. So, correction, my husband is Rev. Dr. David Moore, Pastor. He had already been Pastoring five years when we got married.

The only reason I returned home was because Big Mama left me her house. I had gotten used to city living, but after a while, I couldn't afford living in New York - not in a decent place anyway.

I didn't want to come back to a slow town that was not growing. Everyone knew everyone else's business, and if you weren't careful, you could have ended up dating or marrying one of your relatives! That's how small this town was.

Shoot, Big Mama's house was paid for, so I came back home. When I got back, everyone was telling me about David being a big preacher now. He was not married and had no children. He Pastored one of the largest black churches in our town; it was a step away from being a mega church.

When I had gotten back home, the town had truly changed. There was more than one high school, middle school, and elementary school now. There were even head starts and daycare centers. There was even more than one stop light!

One day after I got back in town, I decided to go see what the talk was about at Pastor David's church.

When I entered the doors of the church, the sanctuary was spectacular. The choirs behind the pulpit were massive. Yes, I said choirs. There was even a balcony. All the seats were filled.

As the ushers guided me to a vacant seat, I was in amazement. David took the old church that his father had, renovated it, and modernized it. I couldn't believe that this was the same church he grew up in. I couldn't believe this was where I came as a little girl with Big Mama to fellowship.

There were about eight chairs on the pulpit. I couldn't quite make out David at first. After all the singing was over and the offerings were collected, it was preaching time. That's when David stood up. Wow, he had changed. He was all grown up now. He did look like his father. His father had been the talk of the town back then because of how good looking he was. He was one of those mixed blacks. You know mixed with a little of this and a little of that.

That's what I had heard when I was a little girl.

The ladies in the church used to go crazy for his father. Huh, I could imagine that they were going on about David now too.

Well, I didn't go to church for that. I went to hear a word from The Lord. The service was good and uplifting. Prior to the end of the service, one of the ushers informed Pastor David that I was there. He made an announcement for me to stand. That was the custom of the church. If you were a visitor you would stand so the church congregation could welcome you.

I wasn't going to stand at first because I didn't consider myself a visitor. I used to come to this church, well not exactly this church, but I came here when his father was the pastor.

I stood anyway. David and I locked eyes and smiled. He still had that smile. Oh, that smile would make you say yes to anything he would ask you to do.

The next thing I saw was him going to the piano and requesting that I give a closing song. He played one of the songs that we used to sing when we were younger, "His Eyes Are on the Sparrow."

I was so nervous. I wasn't sure if I would remember the words. As I got closer to him, he whispered to me, "Don't you be afraid."

When David started playing that piano with the way he made that piano scream, The Holy Spirit came over me, and I began to sing that song as when we were younger. The entire church stood.

After service, I was told by his congregation that it was the best closing of service they ever had.

David requested to meet him in his study after he finished greeting his congregation on their way out of service.

One of the ushers directed me to his study where I waited for about forty-five minutes. He had pictures on the wall of his mom, dad, and awards that were given to him by various community networks for his services and contributions. There were all his degrees on display to let all know that he had surely studied to show himself approved (Oh, that was something I've read in The Bible).

Then, I saw a picture that was black and white and kind of fading. It was of him and me at one of the church picnics. Oh my, I was so skinny in that picture. I had pigtails with ribbons. I laughed so hard.

Why in the world would he have that picture on his desk? Who in the world took that picture? I didn't even remember that day. But seeing it sure brought back fond memories of how we grew up in the South, a far cry from the life and style of New York.

David finally came into his study.

"I'm sorry. I make it a habit to greet everyone who comes to the service. On a bad day, that's nearly two hundred plus people!"

I nodded and let him know that it wasn't a big deal.

"Why don't we get out of here and go get something to eat so we can catch up on old times?"

I looked into his face, and he smiled at me so automatically I said yes. However, before we left I had to know something.

"How did you get that picture of us, and why is it on your desk?"

He just smiled and grabbed my hand; then, we left.

We went to a new upscale restaurant that had opened up in town. David hadn't changed one bit. I asked all about him and what he was doing in past years. He asked about me. We shared with one another what went on in our past and the desires for our future.

"So why weren't you ever married?" I asked him.

"Well, when I was younger, I recall telling a certain young girl that *she* was going to be my wife," he said with a smile.

I looked at him and laughed. I realized at that moment that I had a bit of an attitude, presumably from my interactions in New York.

Right away, I pulled myself together.

"And I recall that I told him that I was never going to marry a PK," I said clearing my throat.

David looked into my eyes, held my hand, and said, "I am not a kid anymore."

Huh, I guess he told me.

"Why do you think I have that picture of us in my study? I knew in my heart that you were the one for me even back then. That picture kept me praying for you while you were gone. I prayed for your safety, your health, and well-being. I was praying for us that one day God would allow you to return, and He did. Yes, I dated in college and since I became a pastor. Those other women were not who I wanted. I knew most of them wanted me because I was a PK. So, I continued with my education and stayed focus on what I wanted. And now my prayers have been answered. The prayers of the righteous does avail much."

That's Bible. I don't even recall eating dinner that night.

Next thing I knew, David and I were getting married. We dated for about three months before we actually got married. My wedding day was a bitter sweet moment for me. I wished that Big Mama was living to see me get married to a Pastor and become a First Lady. The only family I had were some people whom I befriended in New York and Penny.

Penny and her husband flew in from Atlanta for the wedding. Penny was living in Atlanta with her husband who was also a Pastor. I guess Big Mama knew what she was talking about when she said that Penny and I would become First Ladies one day. Penny was my maid of honor.

Our marriage was going very well. We didn't want for anything. David owned most of the town because of all the land and property that his parents left him.

We had two boys, and I was a stay-at-home mom. I wanted to utilize my college education, but David didn't want me to work. He wanted me to stay home with the children. He didn't want anyone else taking care of our children.

"My mother stayed home and took care of me, and you will stay home and take care of our children," he insisted. "My father didn't allow my mother to work, and I won't allow you to work either. The Moore men take care of their women and children."

I argued that back then his mother didn't have a choice, but I had an education, and I could help bring in more income for the family. David wouldn't hear of it. All my fancy clothes, the big house, and expensive cars were all bought for me by my husband.

He did allow me to go shopping for the boys except with the money he gave to me. The boys and I wanted for nothing. The church was doing very well, and David had just opened up a school for grades K through 12 at the church.

I would press the issue that I could run the programs for the schools and reminded him that education is what I had my master's degree in.

David was an only child and true to form, a PK. He was stubborn and insisted on having things his way. He would not hear of me working, even in the church.

Being the good Christian wife, I had to listen to my husband. I would ride to church in the big fancy car that David drove to each service. Every Sunday, I would sit right up front with my fancy dresses, my hats, and matching shoes and pocketbook. On a real fancy day, I would adorn gloves to match!

In the beginning of our marriage, before I had the boys, David allowed me to sing in the choir. However, once I had the boys, he wanted me to sit up front to take care of them. There was a private usher appointed to help me with whatever I needed while at church. If I was going to the restroom, she was there with me.

David even gave me an office so when I needed to feed the boys I could go into my office. The sign on the door read:

First Lady Moore

There was even a parking spot for me that also read:

First Lady Moore

I didn't even need it because most of the time David would drive anyway. While in public, David didn't want me to do anything. When there were functions at the church, I wanted to help in the kitchen or help with anything, but again David wouldn't hear of it. Even the people at the church were conditioned to believe that I couldn't help out with anything.

Although I was waited on hand and foot and was lavished with gifts from the church members, I began to feel that it was what I deserved as the First Lady.

No one understood the life I lived but me. They didn't walk in my fancy expensive shoes.

They didn't know what I put up with and how I *really* felt about being unable to do for myself. So, if they too wanted to take care of me, why not?

I had a husband that loved me, and I knew he meant well. I had two children that were my world, yet I felt alone.

Who could I really talk to about my marriage situation? There was no one I could think of who wouldn't tell the whole church. There was no one I trusted who wouldn't tell the whole town! *No way*, I decided. *I will just tell it to my Lord.*

When David and I were at home, I could do everything: cook, clean, sing, and even go to the bathroom on my own. David would spend a lot of time in his study. At first, I didn't feel any way about that because I knew he had to study for his next sermon and be in constant prayer for the church.

So, most days, the boys and I were alone.

I was living in a house with people, yet it felt empty. David had a large congregational flock to which he had to attend. He would get calls about someone who had died, someone who was in the hospital, or something going on at the school or in the community. No matter what time of day or night it would be, Pastor David was asked to be there. I found myself practically raising the boys on my own.

David was never home.

It seemed like when we did get together, it was to go to church. David did make it his duty to eat Sunday dinner as a family, but only if there was nothing going on after church. It seemed as if every Sunday some type of program was going on after church, so most of the time we ate at the church.

It had gotten to where David and I were less intimate. I wanted more children, but David was so into his ministry.

That is how his congregation had grown over the years, because of him being dedicated to them, or so he thought.

I believe that God allowed me to have two children, so they could keep me company, and that they did. The boys and I did everything together. It was hard for them to listen to their dad because he was hardly around. When David would tell the boys something to do, they would look at me and ask me if it would be ok. David would get upset and remind them who their father was.

When the boys became teenagers, I taught them how to drive. I taught them how men were supposed to be. Although I grew up with Big Mama, I taught them how men were supposed to be based on what I didn't want in a man. Perhaps I was wrong, but I did the best I could because David was hardly around.

I was always faithful to David, and I believe that David had been faithful to me. I had no reason to doubt him. David was just caught up in his ministry. I often wondered if this was the way he had grown up. I wonder if he lived his entire childhood with his mother taking care of him because his dad was a Pastor. I guess that was where he got his loving ways. I often asked myself how could a Pastor be there for everyone else, his congregation, the community, and not be there for his family?

For seventeen years, David and I held our marriage together.

The boys were heading off to college.

David and I had been doing the same things. I went to church with my husband, sat on the front row, and continued to wear my fancy dresses, shoes, and hats. I even carried the pocketbook to match, and on a good day, I would adorn the matching gloves.

I remembered that when I was a little girl I said I would never be a First Lady because it seemed like they couldn't praise The Lord because of their fancy clothes. It wasn't that at all. It was because they were lonely inside.

They were dressed up on the outside and hurting and lonely on the inside. That was me. That was what I had become.

I had everything I could ever want, but I was lonely. I had a husband who loved and took care of me, but I was lonely.

People waited on me hand and foot, yet I was lonely.

Now, that the boys were going off to college, who would be with me?

Who would have thought that I, once such a free and independent, educated woman, would end up like this? I guess it was for love.

After the boys went off to college, David allowed me to go visit Penny in Atlanta. She had fallen ill. I hadn't seen Penny since my wedding, and I needed a break, but most of all I needed someone with whom I could talk.

I was at a breaking point of loneliness in my life. I had kept the secret all this time. I was afraid to divorce him, because I didn't want to look like the bad one or to appear to be ungrateful after all these years.

Why didn't I speak up or speak out earlier?

What should I do?

Who would believe that Pastor David did not show love at home towards his own family when he showed love to others on the outside?

I guess it comes with the territory.

I couldn't wait to see Penny.

Pastor Peter
&
First Lady Penny Taylor

First Lady Penny
The Whole Truth

Dear Diary,

It's me again Penny. I am in the hospital again. I don't know if I am going to make it out this time. Since my diagnosis of HIV two years ago, I continued to go to church with my head held high just like a First Lady should. It took a lot for me to come to the understanding that I didn't do anything wrong. Now that I'm at the end, I feel like I need to tell the truth, the whole truth, nothing but the truth so help me, God.

"God already knows the truth. He was there when it happened. God promised never to leave my side. He said He would never leave me nor forsake me. Even when I was out there in the world, doing me, God was always there by my side.

I remember growing up in the church, but I broke away as soon I was old enough. I didn't run the streets, but I just didn't go to church. I saw the fakeness of the people in the church. They never liked me anyway because I didn't come from a good family. My mother was on drugs, and I didn't know who my father was. I had six siblings who all were from different men. We basically grew up on our own.

I did like going to church because I felt safe when I could get away from my situation at least for a couple of hours. But as I got older, I saw that the people in the church looked down on me. They said that I was going to end up like my mother.

Where was the love? I thought.

Didn't Jesus say to love everyone?

Haven't we all have sinned and fallen short?

The church folk acted as if they had never done anything wrong in their lives. So, when I got older I stopped going. It was hard, but I did finish high school; then, I got my two-year college degree. I didn't stop there though. I went on to get my cosmetology license.

Owning my own beauty shop had always been a dream of mine. One thing I knew was that black women could be broke, busted, and disgusted, but we would get our hair "did."

I was the first of my mother's children to graduate college. As a matter of fact, I was the only one in our entire family to graduate college. I sure proved those who said I was never *gonna* make it wrong. I worked in other people's shops just to save up enough money to open my own shop.

I partnered with a friend of mine who was a barber. Jerry grew up in the neighborhood too. We both had mothers who were on drugs. People thought that he wasn't *gonna* make it either, but he too proved them wrong. Jerry was in and out of jail in his earlier years. The last time he was in prison, he vowed to change.

Jerry went to barber school and got his license. Now, he and I co-own a booming shop. We opened the shop right in town for all the nay-sayers to look and see what God could do. We called the shop *The True Touch* because Jerry and I kept it real.

We would tell the truth to those who came in the shop whether they wanted to hear it or not. I used to say, "If you don't want the truth, don't ask."

I was tired of the church folk lying to each other. So, every time I got an opportunity, when one of those church folks came in to get their hair done, I would just tell them the truth about life and the *real* God.

I would say, "You all need to stop lying to people as if none of you never did anything wrong. Stop looking down on people. Stop killing the spirit of someone who is seeking out God."

They would tell me I was different because I made it. I pulled myself out of where I came from; oh, how I hated those church folk. I know I shouldn't say hate, but that is how I felt towards them. They acted as if they owned God and could pass Him out to only those they chose.

They would still come to the shop because they knew I could hook up the worst head in town. I knew my stuff, and I did a good job.

Jerry was holding his own as well.

Business was good, and things were going well. I had been dating the same man for four years. After our third year, I became pregnant with our son, Deion. Then, after a year, Deion's father left me for another woman. I found myself being a single parent. I had made a vow to myself that I would not be like my mother. My plan was to be with my baby's daddy, but it didn't work out. I had no intention of having another man in my son's life. I planned to raise my son on my own until he grew up. Besides, I was successful at the time.

Then, all of a sudden, it seemed as if I was dating again. I started dating one of Jerry's clients. I used to see Peter on a regular basis. He would come into the shop twice a week to get a haircut. Peter was about 6ft 9in, dark skin, with his body cut up in the right places, and he had a strong firm butt.

Don't let me talk about his shoe size. You know what they say about men with big feet.

I was mesmerized that this man wanted to date me. He had known what happened to Deion's father. He always showed attention to Deion when he would be in the shop, and when we started dating he always did things geared for Deion to come along so I wouldn't have to leave him with a sitter.

I'm sure I fell for Peter because of how he treated Deion.

Peter was in Seminary. His dream was to be a Pastor one day. Oh well, I just thought we would date until that time came.

People who didn't know Peter and I thought that Deion was his son. Out in public, Peter never said otherwise. He wasn't from Atlanta, and his plans were to go back to his hometown of Chicago.

Many times, we came very close to getting it on. I respected his desire to become a Pastor one day, but I had needs and wants. What I wanted was him.

I couldn't understand at the time how he could pass all **THIS** up?

I would put on the sexiest clothes, thongs, or no clothes at all. I would put on the most sensuous perfumes, but still, Peter wouldn't give in.

"How Peter doing," Jerry would ask. "You put it on him yet girl?"

"Not yet," I said. "But I'm going to get him!"

One day, I did just that. Peter finally gave in right before he graduated Seminary.

He was appointed a church right here in Atlanta. I guess he wanted to get it in before he was appointed. After he graduated, he asked me to marry him. Deion had gotten attached to him, and we had been dating for about three years before all this went down. The wait was worth it.

Oh, my Peter was well endowed...

At our wedding, Jerry was the best man, after all we had the business together, and he had been both of our friends for as long as I could remember. Jerry was always there for Peter and me.

Now don't get me wrong, Jerry was well built himself. He had women come in and out of the salon acting a fool over him. Some of them had to be handcuffed out of the salon; that's how bad it used to get!

People thought that Jerry and I would get together, but I made it a rule early on in my career never to date any co-workers or partners in the business.

My wedding was all that I had dreamed of and the two most important people in my life were Deion and Peter.

Finally, we were truly a family.

Deion didn't mind what other people said; to him, Peter was his dad no matter what. We were happy. Peter continued to treat Deion and I very well. He took care of us with no complaints. The church where Peter was appointed was big. When we got there, there was already a large congregation, and it grew even more. I felt like the shit...all eyes were on me.

The other women were in envy. They didn't know how much work I put in to get this life with Peter. I worked too hard and used my bullet for far too long. I wasn't about to let him go.

However, I should have.

About a year into the marriage, Peter told me or somewhat confided in me that he was indeed gay.

Got damn gay? A waste of a man. A waste of a d--. My sexy chocolate gay?

I didn't see it coming.

Perhaps, I should have known because he took so long to touch me. Another clue was after we got married, he consummated the marriage, and that was it.

I just thought we were so busy and didn't have time for each other, and before I realized it, days, months, and years had gone by.

Divorcing Peter was out of the question because he said that I or we would lose everything. He wanted Deion and I to be his front. He was now aspiring to become Bishop one day. He promised to take care of Deion and I. Besides we were already living very well.

Peter told me that I could have another man as long as I kept it on the low. He told me if the church found out that he would divorce me and make it appear as if I was the one who went outside of the marriage.

I couldn't believe my ears. I had already put seven years of my life into this marriage and seven years into the church with those church folk.

I was happy that I was a First Lady who had it all.

Now, I see I sure had it all alright, right down to having HIV.

I was so stupid. I was caught up with trying to prove people wrong. I was telling people that I was all about the truth when all the time I was lying to myself.

Of course, Jerry knew. Jerry actually knew before I did. He told me that Peter had told him just before he told me. He said that Peter wanted to get his advice. Jerry told me that, after some time, Peter was tired of living a lie.

But, he informed Jerry first?

Peter also said that he wanted me to stay in the marriage anyway.

I never told Deion. He was growing up into such a strong responsible man. Deion became so faithful in the church. He used to tell me that he wanted to be just like his father...Peter.

In my mind, I would say to myself, "No you don't." Still, I never said a word.

Long ago in my life, I would have said something, but I never said a word. I guess I became one of those church folks who were living a lie, hiding behind the church, The Bible, and the clothes, yet living a lie just to save face.

I never saw Peter with his lover/man or whatever he called it or him, but I knew he was with someone.

After I was diagnosed, Peter and I told the church folk that I had cancer. I even told Deion that I had cancer. I just didn't want his hopes and dreams to be crushed with the reality of life and its untruths in the world.

I often wondered why and how Peter wasn't diagnosed. The doctor told me that I had HIV right around the time I had sex with Peter for the 1st time. I should have kept my legs closed then. Perhaps, he wouldn't have asked me to marry him. I look back now; I should have kept it moving when he didn't want to have sex all that time. I actually thought it was because he was so faithful to his faith and because of something they were teaching him in Seminary. I guess they were teaching him how to fake it until he made it.

While I was sick in the hospital Peter was out doing his duties as Bishop. Yes, he became a Bishop. His dreams came true.

My son is now an ordained preacher. His dreams of wanting to be just like Peter came true too.

Deion does have a girlfriend. I did ask him at one point down the line if he was attracted to men. He assured me that was not his way. He said he loved women, and that he did. Deion has had many women. I just pray that he settles down with the right woman and remains true to himself and to her or I might never get to see my grandchild.

Why? Because I never said a word.

I remember reading a verse in The Bible that says, "What profits a man to gain the whole world and lose his soul?" That is what I have done. I did make it to be the First Lady of an entire denomination, but I lost my soul just for recognition.

In my dream, I wanted to prove to others that I could become somebody and that I could make it. That I did and look at me now. Look at where I ended up.

One thing I did gain out of all this is to open up my mouth. Never will I be silent as long as I have it in black and white.

Eventually, I did find out who Peter's lover was and still is.

After all these years. I never ever would have thought it...

This is the truth, the whole truth, and nothing but the truth so help me God."

***

Penny paused for a while to catch her breath. There was an oxygen tube inserted in her nose to aid her in breathing.

I sat there in stunned silence.

After Penny had told me all that, I didn't know what to think. I felt hurt and angry at the same time. I just let her express herself due to her condition. I knew she needed someone to talk to; she needed someone to release all that baggage before she released her spirit from her sickly flesh.

I knew that was what was weighing her down for a long time. Penny did not need that to be holding her here on this earth In her eyes I saw that a burden was lifted off of her shoulders once she told me everything.

She asked me not to tell her son the real reason why she was in this situation now.

Penny was always small, but my God, she was so small that I didn't recognized her at first. I never thought that someone could get that small and still survive.

Truly, it was God who was keeping her alive. Her face was so dark. Penny always had color to her, but not like that. That disease had truly taken over her body.

She didn't want any of the congregants to visit her, only her husband and son. She only let me come because I called her and told her that I was coming.

Penny and I went way back. I never sat in judgment of her. I considered us as sisters. Who would have thought that when we were little kids going to church with my Big Mama and being prepped to become a First Lady, we would end up like this?

I thought to myself, "After it's all said and done, we will all end up like this on our death bed."

At the end of the day, it comes to this.

What were all the ups and downs, fussing, and fighting through life really for when this is what it comes to?

I tried to hold back my tears, but I just got a hold of Penny and started to cry. She was consoling me.

I'm not sure if I was crying for her or for myself. Perhaps, I was crying for all the things that a First Lady goes through, and we don't say a word.

Penny thought I was crazy.

"That's why I didn't want no visitors," she said. "Hell, I should be the one crying, but

I'm not. My son is old enough to care for himself. The business has been very profitable, and I have a good life insurance policy. I want to go. I want to finally see our Creator's face and meet Jesus. I want to know if what I got saved for is really real. I want to know by me keeping quiet and keeping the faith that there is really a Heaven. I'm tired. I'm so tired of hurting and fighting. I'm just tired. Everything in my life I have done was because I was told to do, made to do, or forced to do. But now, it has come a time that I am doing something I want to do. I know that there are medications out here today that could keep me going, but for what? A couple of more years? Who knows? But God! I want to go. I have released myself. I have given myself away, and it's ok. I'm ok. It will be ok."

Once Penny had said it that way, a peace came over me. This is what she wants.

She was ok with what was about to happen. Regardless of how it happens, she was ok with it. I saw it in her face, a face of peace.

This is what we as Christians sing about, preach about, and shout about - going to Heaven, but one thing they don't stress is *how* to get there. The only way is by way of death of the flesh, meaning being dead.

It means no longer being able to talk, hear, or feel your family.

I saw that Penny was ready.

So, I fixed myself up, cleaned my face, and felt happy. As I was doing so, Penny dozed off for a little while. I let her rest because I knew she needed it. As she slept, I continued to read her diary which she had said would be ok. Besides, she had told me once she had read it to me that she wanted me to keep it.

She didn't want the truth to be buried with her, but for me to keep it to teach others as well as for me to teach myself. As I continued to read, I noticed that she left out who Peter was seeing. I wondered if Peter was seeing a woman who was in the church. That's how those women are, always wanting the Pastor.

Why? I don't know.

Maybe, it is for the reputation or the status, but if they only knew the real deal.

As I was approaching the last page, Penny woke up. She just started talking and continued where she left off as if she hadn't fallen asleep.

She hadn't eaten or drank anything but was wanting some ice chips to soother her dry mouth.

As I went to get the ice, I wondered why Peter wasn't there with her or why her son wasn't either. You would figure the Bishop would be here knowing his wife was about to pass away.

On my way to get the ice, I stopped in the chapel to say a prayer. I wanted to pray not for Penny only but for myself and my family. Times like these make a person appreciate more and more of what they have in life. I realized that every moment with your loved one counts because we just don't know the day nor the hour we will be called to the other side.

No more would I complain of what I don't have or what I don't get.

From now on, I would appreciate what I do have and make the best of it. I thanked God for what He has given to me. I thanked God for the many valleys He has seen me through. To God be the Glory for all that He has done. I thanked God that Penny was not suffering at this time.

When I went back to Penny's room, the nurse was just now leaving.

"I just gave her something for the pain," the nurse said.

"What did you give her?" I asked.

"Morphine," she responded and continued to the nurse's station. "Let us know if she needs anything further."

When I walked into the room, Penny was asleep again. I made myself comfortable on the bay window which was also the bed area, and I too went to sleep.

I woke up to a loud sounding noise. The lights were on and a lot of people were in the room.

When I got my bearings, I realized that Peter and Penny's son were there by her bed. Her son was crying, and I knew then that Penny had passed.

She didn't even alert me. She just went in her sleep. There I was asleep too, but I woke up.

I got up and held her son as he cried. I didn't say much to Peter at the time. Penny's son handed me her diary and said that his mother wanted me to have it. I thought to myself, "She didn't get to tell me who Peter was seeing." Then, I had another thought. "If it were for me to know, she would have told me."

They allowed us to look upon her face one more time before they put the sheet over her.

As they were gathering up Penny's belongings she brought to the hospital, I asked Peter why he wasn't here earlier.

He informed me that Penny said she was going home tomorrow so there was no need for him or her son to come and sit around when they could be doing other things. He said she told them to come get her in the morning and that they indeed came to do. Penny had passed away around 3am when the hospital called to notify them of her passing. No one woke me up.

They said that when the nurse had checked on her and gave her the last pain medication, Penny told her that if I had fallen to sleep not to wake me because I had come from a long way and needed the rest. So, they did as Penny said.

I left with Peter to go to the funeral home. On our way there, I started to read Penny's diary from where I left off and when I got to the last page, I couldn't believe what I was reading.

Penny wrote:

I will now speak the truth and nothing but the truth, so help me God. I saw Peter and his lover one afternoon leaving our house. Before they departed into their own cars, they hugged and kissed as if they had been lovers for a long time. It hurt my heart to the core. I got sick to my stomach, but I never said a word until now.

Peter's lover is Jerry...

Rest in Peace

First Lady Penny Taylor

January 18, 1960 – March 28, 2005

Pastor Johnathan
&
First Lady Dana Johnson

First Lady Dana
Cheaper to Keep Her

I can't believe it's twenty years today that Johnathan and I got married. Just to think all those who said we weren't going to make it, but we did. Look at us now, still together.

Although we have slept in separate rooms for years, Johnathan is still my husband.

He knows *it's cheaper to keep her*. At least that is what they say.

I am proud to say that I have been First Lady for the past twenty years. We have moved from several churches and cities, but it has been twenty years. I know one thing; I am not going to give up my position without a price, a big price at that!

Johnathan knows I just might take some people with me too.

If I go down, a lot of people will go down with me!

But that's not going to happen any time soon. I still do my thing on the side if you know what I mean.

Why not?

Johnathan and I haven't slept in the same room, let alone the same bed, for the past nineteen years. So, when I need a fix I go out and get it.

I'm sure he does the same thing because he's not getting any from me, unless he is gay which I highly doubt, or he does himself.

Johnathan was already preaching when I met him. He acted like he was holier than thou in front of the congregation, but when he came over to my house, he sure didn't think about the church I tell you that.

Oh, my! It used to be so good, so hot, and sexy when we started.

His tall slender body on top of mine feeling, his sweat between my legs, and his big thang made me wet before we even got started. He was like a beast.

This went on even after he got his church. No one knew I was with him then. I sure wasn't cut out to be a First Lady I tell you that. I not only had Johnathan, but when he didn't come through for me I sure had a backup. I always did. I still do now.

In fact, I have been with the same man just as long as I have been with Johnathan. He understands my situation. He has someone, and so do I. We both agreed that we will not leave our spouses. Besides, *it is cheaper to keep her*.

That's what they say.

Nevertheless, we just do what we do. While Johnathan goes out and does his Pastor thing, I go out doing mine if you know what I mean.

But on Sunday mornings, I am there with my dress, hat, shoes, and gloves to match, sitting up front just as a First Lady should and pray God's forgiveness.

I try to live right. I try to live holy, but it's hard for me. I didn't want this position. The only reason why Johnathan and I got married in the first place is because I got pregnant. Of course, he had to cover up his mess. How would it look to know the Pastor has a child out of wedlock? Not for Johnathan, he wasn't about to lose all he had worked hard for.

So, here we are twenty years later.

I say to myself at times that we are just living a lie. It's just a sin to live in a lie. It's just as bad to stay in one. I know over the years that Johnathan has had his share of women right in the church. Some of them I would talk to, smile, and break bread with knowing that they were sleeping with my husband.

Of course, he kept his nose clean. He would deny it up and down when I would confront him about it. It got to the point that I just told him he better not come home with any babies, and no one better not call my house.

That's why every Sunday I would wear my Sunday best, yes, my hat, gloves, shoes, and purse to match. I would strut my stuff right to the front row knowing all eyes were on me, even the ones that Johnathan had slept with and with whom he was still sleeping. Those women were fools. I know each one of them thought that they were the only one. Johnathan played them all, sometimes at the same time.

One time I picked up the phone while he was talking to one of them. She was the Deaconess of the church, and they weren't talking about church business either.

I knew they all were jealous of me; that's why I did that. I made sure they would know that I was the one getting served at the Pastor's table. I was the wife who was recognized before each sermon. I was the one who was getting the gifts at each anniversary, not them. I would just smile, speak softly, and keep it moving. I knew they wanted to be in my shoes, but they couldn't have them.

Word would get to me about who Johnathan was sleeping with and going out with, but I knew he wasn't going anywhere. "How could he?" He was about to lose everything, and I mean everything. I knew too many of his secrets. Besides, I wouldn't even remarry at my age, so he would have to pay me alimony for the rest of my life or at least a good part of my remaining years.

My man and I would just live off of his money; knowing Johnathan, he would die first before he takes care of another man.

I know I am a sinner, but I have looked at Johnathan all these years and wondered how *he* could look at himself in the mirror. "How could he teach people right from wrong? How could he teach the truth from lies, when he is living a lie himself?"

I'm reminded of a scripture somewhere in The Bible where Jesus told someone that He knew them not after the man said to Jesus that he did works in His name.

I see that will be Johnathan.

I have told him that he is a hypocrite. His response to me is always the same:

"God knows my heart."

Well, God knows mine too. God knows that I am a woman and that I have needs. Johnathan had a woman in every church we have attended. He must think that I didn't know, but I knew everyone and every time.

There is one woman who has been with Johnathan just as long as we were together. They are longtime friends who grew up together. She has a family as well, but that has never stopped anyone. I just go along with the program.

Besides, when he goes on the prowl, it allows me to go on mine. He has his excuses, and so do I. My girlfriends or my sister are my excuses. Don't get me wrong; I love Johnathan perhaps because

Rochelle Pearson
97

we were together for so long or because we are just alike.

"Could he be my soulmate?"

He allows me to do me, and I allow him to do him. God would be the judge.

WOW!! Twenty years today and I'm here at home getting myself together to meet Johnathan. Yes! For our twentieth anniversary, I got him some flowers, and I am going to pick up a cake. Our daughter is going to join us. She is going to pick up his favorite food from the Chinese restaurant and get some balloons.

I went into Johnathan's room to get his favorite suit with a tie that he likes. He always looks good in this dark blue tie with light blue stripes. I got the blue and silver cufflinks he likes as well. My husband is going to look good today.

Although it wasn't Sunday, I put on my Sunday best. I still look good honey! I've been working out. I have always kept myself up, especially for being the First Lady! Now, I was ready to go meet Johnathan, I told him that we were coming.

I was not sure if he would have remembered. I know he was waiting all day. I am running behind as usual. I called him and let him know I was on my way. My daughter had gotten to him before I did. She was grown and living on her own now.

I know if I ever did anything right in my life, my daughter was it. She never gave us any problems. She graduated college, got a good job, and got her own apartment. She is holding her own. I know she doesn't play men running in and out of her place.

That's one thing she didn't take from her father or me. I thank God for her. As I arrived to where Johnathan and our daughter were, they were already in the dining area. She had started serving the Chinese food to her father. I had wanted him dressed before we ate. I guess he couldn't wait. Johnathan always liked Chinese food.

I presented the flowers and cake to Johnathan. I knew he was happy although he was unable to show it.

Johnathan had a stroke last year. He is now paralyzed on his left side. He now has slurred speech. He hasn't been able to preach since his stroke. After our daughter helped her father to eat, I had her to help me take him back to his room to put on his clothes that I had brought him. He still liked to dress up in his suits. Johnathan can't dress himself anymore.

The rehab facility had allowed us to use the private dining area for our anniversary celebration. We cleaned and dressed him and went back to the dining area. He looked and smelled good now.

Johnathan is unable to go to the bathroom on his own. He now wears briefs or diapers if you will. At times, he needs help with his personal hygiene. I know if Johnathan could help it he would die knowing he has on briefs and needs to be changed. I wonder what he is thinking. He just stares. They are giving him speech therapy, but all he says now is yes or no.

He might shake his head every now and then.

It hurts my heart to see him like this. I visit him every day when I am able. When this happened, all the women who wanted him and were with him scattered. I never seen anyone of them come up here to wipe his ass, feed him, or dress him. He is no use to them now I guess.

"What was it all for?" I ask myself. When we are in the prime of our lives, we fail to think that if we live long enough, we get older. We may or may not get sick. We lose our youthful looks. Body parts begin to sag. Some of us have to get medication to help get the sex drive back that we use to have when we were younger.

As I look back over my life, I realized that it has come to this. At the end of it all I asked myself, "Was it worth it?"

As it is written in The Bible, "There is a time and season for everything under the sun." Now, it was time for our daughter and me to go.

Most times, after Johnathan eats, he is ready to go to bed. Besides, they have him up so early in the morning. Now, he is on a routine. He gets up by 6:00am and has breakfast at 7:30am every day. This is what it has come to for him.

Well, it's not that way for me; thank God.

I don't know what happened, but I know God got a hold of me. Right after Johnathan had his stroke, I was so afraid. Reality set in. I knew God was real, no, really real then. I said to myself that God took Johnathan's speech because of all the sinful things he was doing and proclaiming in His name. I just knew that I was going to be next. After all, I wasn't a saint.

So, I went to church on that Sunday. The Assistant Pastor had to preach.

Of course, as usual, I walked right to the front with my hat, dress, gloves, and shoes to match and sat in my seat. I couldn't remember what the preacher was preaching about. All I remember is before he had finished his sermon, I began to cry out and holler uncontrollably. The congregation thought I was doing so for Johnathan because he just had a stroke.

I heard them say, "Leave her alone; she is praying and crying for her husband.

Don't touch her. Let her cry; she needs to pray for her husband."

Little did they know that I was praying for myself!

I did pray for Johnathan too, but it was mostly for me. I just didn't know what came over me. All the anger I had let set within me for all those years had to be released. I realized at that moment that it wasn't necessary. I realized that I allowed Johnathan's sins and those other women's sins of what they were doing to become my sins because I went out to do the same things.

At that very moment, I asked God to take it all away. I repented of my sins.

See, I realized that I was going to have to give an account of my deeds and not anyone else's. After all the years of being in church and going to church, I was acting the part of church. I wasn't saved.

At that moment, I gave myself totally and fully to God. I surrendered all. I didn't care who saw me.

There I was, makeup running down my face, shoes off, gloves off, hat in the seat, hair messed up, brand new dress and all prostrated on the floor of the church before The Lord.

When I did get up after some time, which felt like a life time, the past didn't matter anymore. I felt a change come over me. I felt like a new person. To me it felt better than sex, which I had thought at one time that sex, especially good sex, was the all and all. But now, I know different. Jesus' Holy Spirit in my life is my All in All.

A change came over me. A wonderful change came over me. Next thing I knew, I was preaching. I became a Pastor. I used to be on the streets committing adultery while being known as the First Lady.

It seems as if the table had changed. Now, I am the Pastor. I felt badly that Johnathan couldn't speak. I wonder what he is saying in his head.

With the way he used to treat me and what he used to call me, I know if he could speak, he would let me know that I can't preach. He would tell me that it was all make believe. Long as I know that I know, that I know. I do know that this joy that I have, the world didn't give it to me, and the world can't take it away.

After some time, I did make accommodations for Johnathan to come home, wheelchair accessibility, shower safety, etc. After all he was still my husband and the father of our daughter. God's love that I felt within outweighed all the hurt, cheating, and pain that I ever felt from Johnathan in the past.

Johnathan came home, and I saw a new man. I fell in love with my husband all over again. It wasn't about the sex anymore. It was about seeing how God worked miracles through Johnathan. Day by day, I saw how real God really is.

Slowly, Johnathan started to regain his strength through his speech and his ability to walk with a walker. I noticed when he would accomplish what the Physical Therapist would put before him, his brown eyes would shine. It was something new to me that I have never seen before in him. I felt like I was married to a new man, a different man.

"Who was this new Johnathan?"

Meanwhile at church, new growth was increasing. I know that it was The Holy Spirit. I was preaching truth and being real with the people. Most of all, I showed real love towards the people, and they began to tell others.

One Sunday, there were twenty people whom I counted that gave their lives to Christ. It could have been more, but God only knows.

As I looked back over my life, I realize that God had my life already mapped out for me, whether good or bad. My experiences I had encountered helped others whom were going through the same things that I did in my past. To God be the Glory!

Then, one day, the very same man whom I was dealing with way back when, came into the church, he and his wife. I had never met her. But at that time, I didn't care to meet her. Anyway, as I was sitting on the pulpit about to go up to preach, here they came walking in. All of a sudden, my past issues, sins, feelings, and emotions popped up. I felt as if I wanted him again, but I had to put my flesh into submission. I had to act as if I didn't even know him.

I was able to preach without interruption as The Holy Spirit interceded. I went to the back of the church to meet and greet as I normally do.

Then, here they both came. He shook my hand and she, the wife, hugged me and told me that my sermon touched her heart. She, then, asked if I would give them counseling.

Right off the bat, I said yes. I was a servant of The Lord. I, then, had them meet with my secretary to set up an appointment. I didn't know how to feel or what to think. My ex-lover, my old lover, my used to be sex partner and his wife want counseling. "What in the world am I to do?" I knew for sure that I did not have any more feelings for him. Once I had repented and giving it all over to God, I had no desire to do what I used to do, but I knew that I was not one hundred percent in where I wanted to be. Still, I wasn't what I used to be.

That week I went into fasting and praying. I wanted to tell Johnathan of what was going on to perhaps get feedback, but he wasn't fully recovered. He still had problems expressing himself without getting angry, but I wanted to confide in my husband.

I didn't know how he would take it knowing I had a lover as long as we had been married. I asked myself if it was the right time to tell him the truth of the days of old. Besides, he never told me of his many love affairs. I often wondered if he would have told me had he not had a stroke. "Would he confess to me once he is able?"

Although I knew and have always known, I would like to hear him confess. Perhaps, in some ways, I see how God feels with us confessing with our mouths that He indeed raised Jesus from the dead (Romans 9:10). It's something about confessing with your mouth, just to hear the words of the things that you knew were going on or the things that you knew were true all along.

That week seemed like the longest week of my life. I knew I was a new creature in Christ. All my sins had been forgiven, or so I hoped.

The day had finally come when I had to meet with Dexter and his wife, Angel.

What a name! Angel.

Anyway, I got to my office in the church an hour early and began practicing what I was going to say. I brushed up on notes and thought on questions they might ask me since it was marriage counseling, and I had some idea of how things would go.

I made sure, on that day, to wear a long skirt, a shirt, and jacket that didn't show any of my skin. I said to myself that it shouldn't matter. Dexter had seen every part of me possible, but I knew it was a new me, a new day. Besides, they asked me to counsel them. They came to my church. They were the ones needing help.

I had long since handed it over to God. I pulled out all sorts of scriptures to help with this marriage counseling. I had to turn the AC unit down, I was sweating so much. This was the first time that I wished that I was not a Pastor. I wished that Johnathan were here instead of me. I'm sure he would have known how to BS his way through it all.

Maybe, it was a test to see how far I had come in my faith. Maybe Dexter's wife was trying to see if I was really saved. I did plan to tell her that I was sorry if I had offended her in any way in the past. I was going to let her know that I had an affair with her husband for many years, but it was when I was out there in the world. He didn't mean anything like that to me now. I wanted her to know that I was a changed woman by the Grace and Mercy of God.

I thought to myself, "What have I done to deserve this now? I have been faithful in spite of Johnathan's illness. I had forgiven my husband since I had been forgiven by God. I had even forgiven myself. I had moved on.

The church is growing, I have a large congregation that loves me and loves The Lord." I asked myself, "Why am I in this position right now?"

As I was meditating, I heard a noise. I looked up I saw Johnathan coming into the church heading to my office with his Therapist. He was standing by himself while he walked with his walker. I thought to myself, "Here comes the tall, sexy, chocolate man that I married." Still, I wondered why they came to the church. I opened my office door and gave Johnathan a hug and a big kiss. Oh, how I wished that we could get back to the way it used to be, but I don't worry about that now because he is my husband, and I am a Pastor.

"Why are you here?" I asked.

"He said he wanted to come over to be here when you meet with Dexter and Angel."

"How do you know I am meeting with them," I asked confused.

In his slurred speech, my husband said, "Angel told me to come. She invited me to sit in on the session."

I thought perhaps she felt that Johnathan was more experienced than I was in counseling and Pastoring.

Before I could respond, Dexter and Angel arrived. I must admit, Dexter still kept himself up. He looked good as ever, but I didn't let that block my duty at hand as the Pastor. I invited them to take a seat.

Johnathan was sitting next to me. I felt proud to have my husband next to me as I conducted business in the service of The Lord. I just wanted Dexter and Angel to find love if they hadn't yet, like Johnathan and I. They just needed to let the past be the past in order to move forward.

As we were all seated, the therapist left the room. I began to ask everyone to hold hands as I began to pray to open up the counseling session. Once I finished praying, I asked if all minds and hearts were clear in order for this counseling session to begin in the truth and the light of honesty, openness and forgiveness.

So, I *thought* I was going to start by confessing my sins to Angel as Dexter sat there in silence, but Angel beat me to the point.

"My two sons are not by my husband. They are Johnathan's sons," she yelled.

Her sons were around the same age as my daughter. She started to cry.

"Johnathan and Dexter have known from day one. My husband is unable to have children, so he accepted the boys as his."

Dexter sat there in silence.

"I called this meeting because I have been diagnosed with stage four cancer, and the prognosis doesn't look good," Angel confessed. "The doctors are saying I only have about three months to live."

You wouldn't have guessed that by the way she looked.

"I know you're a good mother," Angel continued. "I saw how you raised your daughter and how well she has turned out. I have even noticed how well you have taken care of Johnathan during his sickness and even brought him home to care for him instead of leaving him in a facility. I know this is a lot, but I want to know if you will watch out for my boys when I'm gone."

At first, I was shocked. Inside, I wanted to curse, fight, run, or even hide. But, I gained the strength to tell the truth as well.

I informed them that I had a confession of my own.

Johnathan was unable to show any type of expression due to his stroke. Dexter just continued to sit there in silence. I guess he knew that one day the truth would come out.

I looked at Angel, who was holding her husband's hands so tightly, obviously in fear over his reaction to what she had just confessed.

"Angel, your story is not entirely true," I began. "Especially the part about Dexter not being able to have children. My daughter, who everyone believes is Johnathan's child, is actually Dexter's child."

At that moment, I felt freer than I ever felt before. So, I guess it is true; *the truth shall set you free...*

Epilogue

There were a lot of people at Penny's funeral. She had more friends than any of us knew about. It turns out she belonged to a group of First Ladies. They met once a month and talked about the challenges of being First Ladies.

There were two ladies there in particular who were taking things very hard.

One looked very frail and thin. The other looked strong, but her eyes told me that she too was dealing with something that was weighing on her spirit.

I went over to them and introduced myself.

"Hi, my name is Monica. Penny was my best friend."

They told me their names were Dana and Angel.

"Penny was a great friend to me," Angel said. "She told me that I had to find a way to talk to Monica."

Discussion Questions

Why do you think being a First Lady is so coveted?

After reading this story, do you feel differently about the wives of Pastors and ministers? Why or why not?

Do you think the marriage of a First Lady is any different than the marriage of any other woman? Why or why not?

Can you identify with any of the women in this story? How?

In each of these situations, lies were exposed at the end of the relationship. Do you think 'telling the truth' early on would have mattered in these relationships?

If confessing sin to God grants you forgiveness, do you think it is necessary to confess your sins to others? Why or why not?

Penny paid the ultimate price for her silence. Why do you think she kept everyone away when she knew death was near?

Do you think the wives were as much to blame for their failed marriages, or do you think the blame is all of the husband's fault? Explain your response.

Why do you think Dexter and Johnathan were silent during Angel's confession? In your opinion, is it typical for men to remain silent when dealing with on relationship matters?

What are your thoughts about Angel asking Dana to watch over her boys?

About the Author

In her first novel, Rochelle Pearson lifts the 'big fancy hat' First Ladies are known for wearing and reveals the painful truth that plagues many of them. Behind the smiling face, there is a hurting heart.

As truths are revealed, each of the First Ladies discover that the truth really will set you free.

Rochelle is a native New Yorker raised in South Carolina by her grandmother. She knew at an early age that church was the center of all southern households. No matter what a person did from Monday to Saturday, on Sundays, everybody went to church to either confess their truth or hide their lies.

To contact Rochelle Pearson

Email: pearsonproductions1@gmail.com

Facebook: @PearsonProductions1

Word Angels Books

is an imprint of

The Butterfly Typeface Publishing.

Contact us for all your

publishing & writing needs!

Iris M Williams
PO Box 56193
Little Rock AR 72215

www.butterflytypeface.com

www.ingramcontent.com/pod-product-compliance
Lightning Source LLC
Chambersburg PA
CBHW030524260626
47157CB00005B/1874